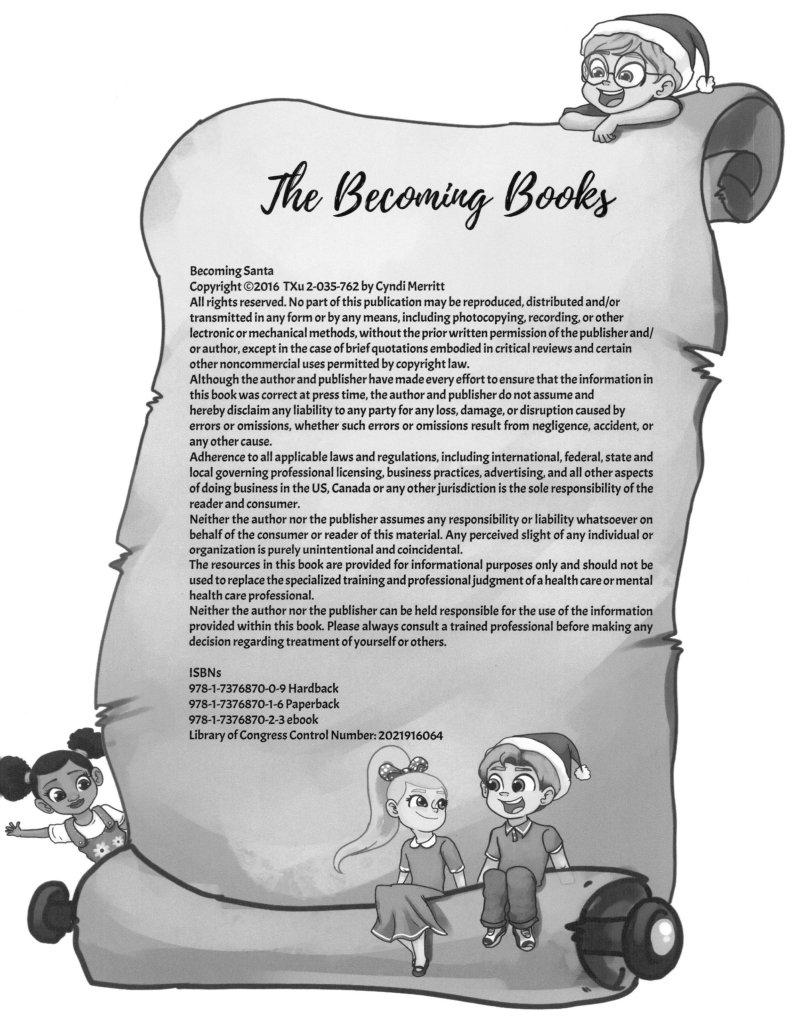

The Becoming Books

ISBNs
978-1-7376870-0-9 Hardback
978-1-7376870-1-6 Paperback
978-1-7376870-2-3 ebook
Library of Congress Control Number: 2021916064

Becoming Santa

For Daniel
and all the future Santas of the world!

Written By Cyndi "Go Go" Merritt

Illustrated By Oliver Kryzz Bundoc

Edited By Matt Cubberly

It was springtime and a baby boy came into the world.
His name was Daniel and his parents
loved him very much.
They were so grateful for him and said Daniel
was truly a gift.

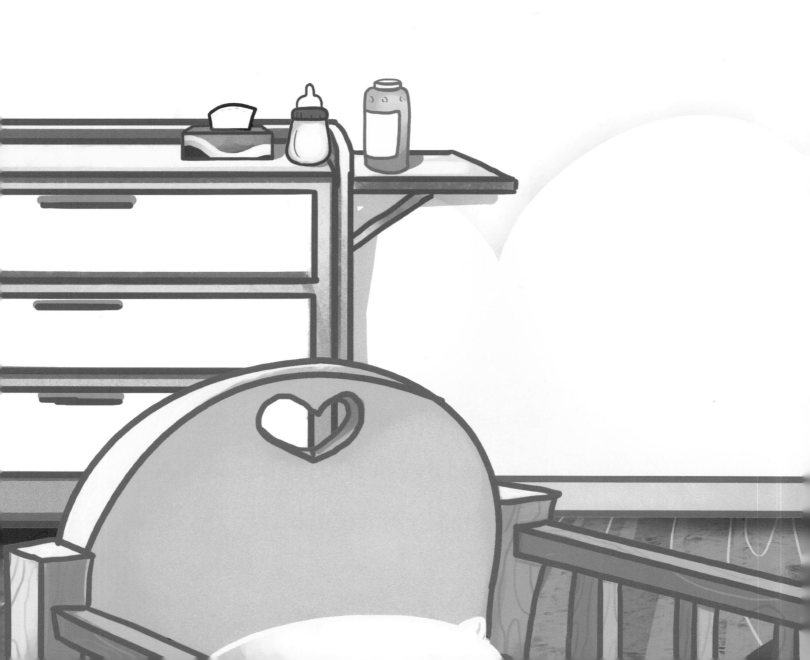

As little boys do, Daniel started to grow and by his first Christmas, he was rolling around the floor and looking up at the beautiful lights on the Christmas tree. Santa came to visit Daniel and brought him gifts wrapped in brightly colored paper and bows.

And as Santa always does, he kissed Daniel's forehead as Daniel slept soundly in his crib.

A few years passed and with each Christmas, Daniel grew smarter and taller and even more handsome. He was big enough now to help his mom and dad decorate the Christmas tree. Santa came to visit Daniel each year and always brought him gifts wrapped in brightly colored paper and bows.

And as Santa always does, he kissed Daniel's forehead as Daniel slept soundly in his bed.

Soon the time came when Daniel was old enough to go to school. He loved school and had lots of friends in his class. Daniel discovered that Santa visited his friends too! They all wrote Santa letters and put milk and cookies out for him on Christmas Eve.

Some of the children even left carrots for Santa's reindeer! It made Daniel happy to know Santa loved all the children in his class and they all loved Santa too.

Another year passed and Daniel was once again excited that Christmas and Santa were coming! He loved the houses in his neighborhood that were all lit up with twinkling Christmas lights. Some houses had white lights, but Daniel liked the colorful lights best. He liked how everyone seemed happier and smiled more this time of year. He especially liked it if it snowed!

Daniel and some of his friends began to notice that they saw Santa in lots of different places. They spotted him at the store, in parades, on television, and even ringing bells on street corners. Santa always looked somewhat the same, but also a little different. It was strange that Santa seemed to be in two - or twenty-two - places at once. It was curious.

Soon it was the last day of school and the class Christmas party was in full swing! It was loads of fun and there were piles of cookies and cupcakes. Everyone sang songs and laughed - everyone except Daniel's friend, Tommy. Tommy simply sat in the corner and watched. Daniel tried to get him to join in the fun, but Tommy just pushed him away.

Everyone said there was trouble in Tommy's house, and he didn't have a dad anymore. Tommy used to be nice, but now he was kind of mean to some of the kids. He started saying that Santa wasn't real and only babies believed in Santa. This made Daniel's heart feel sad and he felt sad for Tommy too because out of all the children in his class, Santa didn't visit Tommy. Daniel wondered why.

At the end of the day, Daniel's mom met him as he got off the school bus and she could tell something was bothering him.

They went inside their house that was decorated with Daniel's favorite colorful Christmas lights. Daniel and his mom sat down for their afternoon snack, but Daniel wasn't hungry. Maybe because of all the cookies and cupcakes from the party, but maybe because he was sad about his friend Tommy.

"Mom, today at the Christmas party, Tommy said Santa isn't real."

"Daniel, you are growing smarter and taller and even more handsome every day, and your heart is growing too. In fact, this year I think your heart has grown enough that you are finally ready!"

"Ready for what, Mom?"

"This year, it's time for you to start becoming

Santa."

"Me? Become Santa? I don't understand!"

"Have you seen Santa in the store and in the parade and on television?"
Daniel nodded his head.
"Well, have you noticed Santa looks a little different each time?"
Daniel shrugged his shoulders, but he had indeed noticed.

"Sometimes, people say that they might be Santa's helpers because even though they are dressed in the red suit and have a beard, they look a little different. Sadly, some children, like your friend Tommy, might even think that Santa isn't real and that those are just people dressed up in a costume."
Daniel grew teary-eyed because that's just what Tommy said.

"Some children say that because they aren't ready to become Santa yet. But Daniel, you are ready! This is the Christmas that you will start becoming Santa!" Daniel took a deep breath and listened closely.

"Santa doesn't always have a red suit and a beard, sometimes he looks just like you and me! You know that wonderful, magical feeling you get deep down inside when you do something nice for someone? That's the feeling that Santa gets every time he visits a child or a family and gives them a special gift. Daniel, do you know anyone who needs some Christmas magic from Santa this year?"

"Yes! Tommy and his mom need some Christmas magic!
Let's go call him!"

"Wait, Daniel. Part of the magic of Christmas and becoming Santa is giving gifts quietly and in secret. Becoming Santa means you never let the person know who you are. Becoming Santa is giving an unselfish gift of hope and love. That is the true spirit of becoming Santa. It means Santa's spirit lives quietly in your heart."

Daniel nodded his head as he started to understand. Then he and his mom began figuring out what gifts he could bring for Tommy and his mom.

Daniel emptied his piggy bank and his mom took him to the store. He bought Tommy some toys and a new pair of gloves. He bought Tommy's mom a bottle of perfume. Daniel's mom helped by purchasing food and a special turkey for their Christmas dinner..

Daniel wrapped the gifts in brightly colored paper and bows and on Christmas Eve, Daniel, his mom, and his dad drove to Tommy's house. There were no colorful Christmas lights on Tommy's house. It was the only dark house on the street. Daniel quietly put the gifts and the bags of food on the front porch. Then Daniel rang the doorbell and ran as fast as he could to hide in the car.

Daniel and his family watched as Tommy and his mom opened the front door to find all the Christmas gifts and the bags of food on the front porch. Tommy's mom cried and kissed Tommy on the forehead, just as Santa would do.

Daniel never told Tommy he was Santa, but knowing made him feel happy inside. Daniel could tell the magical Christmas spirit of Santa was growing in his heart.
Every Christmas after that, Daniel became Santa for someone else. He wrapped gifts in brightly colored paper and bows and delivered them in secret on Christmas Eve.

Daniel grew smarter and taller and even more handsome, and his loving heart grew in the spirit of Santa too. Although they never spoke of it, Daniel suspected that some of his classmates held the spirit of Santa in their hearts too. In time, he could even tell his good friend Tommy had Santa's spirit in his heart.

The years passed and when he was fully grown, Daniel and his wife brought a new baby girl into the world. Her name was Mary. Daniel and his wife loved her very much. They were so grateful for her and said she was truly a gift.

That year, Santa came to visit Mary and brought her gifts wrapped in brightly colored paper and bows.

And as Santa always does, he kissed Mary's forehead
as she slept soundly in her crib.

This is not the end, this is just the beginning.

About the Author

Cyndi Merritt, or "Go Go" as she's known to those that love her, is a Writer, a Realtor and a REALLY Goofy Grandmother! She is a Christian and loves animals, traveling, nature, music and most of all her family and friends. You might find her at the beach, in the mountains or just getting lost somewhere exploring new places. If you're with her, be warned, she will wander off! Her favorite foods are pizza and peanut butter (but not together). Her motto is "Work hard, Play harder, Laugh lots, Live every moment to the fullest, Love with all your heart, and Leave this world a better place."

About the Illustrator

Oliver Kryzz Bundoc is a children's book illustrator based from the Philippines. He is an aspiring artist hoping to provide and help aspiring authors through his illustrations.

Visit www.TheBecomingBooks.com for a free download of Becoming Santa's Scroll so your children can make a list of the people or gifts they would like to share while they Become Santa.